JUL   2015

First published in the United States, Great Britain, Canada, Australia, and New Zealand
in 2015 by NorthSouth Books Inc., an imprint of NordSüd Verlag AG, CH-8005 Zürich,
Switzerland.

Distributed in the United States by NorthSouth Books, Inc., New York 10016.
Library of Congress Cataloging-in-Publication Data is available.
ISBN: 978-0-7358-4207-6

Printed in Germany by Grafisches Centrum Cuno GmbH & Co. KG, Calbe, October 2014
1 3 5 7 9 • 10 8 6 4 2
www.northsouth.com

FSC
www.fsc.org
MIX
Paper from
responsible sources
FSC® C043106

An Aesop Fable

The Tortoise and the Hare

RETOLD AND ILLUSTRATED BY
Bernadette Watts

North
South

One summer day the animals decided to go on a picnic.
They set off across a meadow and settled under a tree.
After the picnic they enjoyed games and races.

Then Tortoise said to Hare, "I bet I can beat you in a
running race!"

Everyone laughed. They all knew how slow Tortoise
walked and how fast Hare ran.

But Hare replied, "Very well, Tortoise, I accept your
challenge."

They agreed that the race should end where it began,
going in a circle, from the tree and back to the tree.

The animals chose a duck to start the race.

"QUACK! QUACK!" shouted Duck.

Everyone cheered! The runners were off!

In less than a minute Hare was across the meadow. He looked back over his shoulder and saw that Tortoise had not even left the shade of the tree.

Hare raced on; he passed a farm without stopping. Then he ran through a golden cornfield. Hare jumped over a stile and into a lane.

Hare looked about but saw no one else in the lane. So he hopped leisurely along, taking his time. "There is no hurry," he said to himself with a smile. "If I walk all the way, I will still win."

Hare came to a cottage. He nipped around
to the back garden where the vegetables grew.
He ate a whole row of lettuce, some carrot
tops, and a large, crisp cabbage.

Meanwhile, Tortoise trudged on, across
the meadow and through the golden corn,
until he reached the stile. He went under the
stile and started to walk along the dusty lane.

Hare spent a long time in the garden, tasting this and nibbling that.

He ate more than enough. He was very, very full. But then he just ate a fallen apple . . . and another apple. . . . He was so full that his stomach bulged out on both sides.

Hare went on until he came to a stream. He took
a long, long drink, as his huge lunch and the hot
day had made him extremely thirsty.

Then he spotted his old friend Mr. Fox sitting
there on the grassy bank of the stream.

Hare and Mr. Fox started talking, and they went
on and on, talking for quite some time like old
friends do.

Tortoise plodded along, slowly but surely.

At last he came to the cottage. Tortoise felt hot and a bit hungry. His short legs felt tired.

But he walked right past the cottage and the gate, which lead to the garden. He wondered where Hare was now.

Hare and Mr. Fox had said good-bye to
each other.

The hare continued on his way. Mr. Fox
went the other way on some errands of his own

Later in the afternoon Hare came to a cornfield,
which had been harvested. A hedge full of honeysuckle
and wild roses grew around the field.

Hare felt very drowsy, so he stopped to rest under
the hedge.

"I have eaten too much," he said to himself.
"There is plenty of time for a nap. Tortoise is far
behind."

Hare stretched out, sighed deeply, and fell asleep.

The heat of the long summer afternoon and the heavy perfume of the flowers had made Hare oversleep. When he awoke, there were long shadows across the grass, and the sun had fallen down behind the wood.

Hare sat up and rubbed his eyes. Where was Tortoise? Hare could not see him in any direction.

Now Tortoise had passed right by Hare sleeping under the hedge. Tortoise heard Hare snoring.

Although Tortoise was hot and tired, he just plodded slowly on.

The little animals who lived on either side of the track came out and cheered him on.

Tortoise walked right around the cornfield without a pause, and went under the gate and back into the meadow. The circle was nearly complete!

Hare sat up in alarm. He looked back along the lane. Tortoise was nowhere to be seen.

Suddenly, in the distance Hare heard all the animals cheering.

Then Hare knew—too late!—what had happened. He sprang up and raced right around the cornfield, under the gate, and back into the meadow.

How the animals cheered!
How Hare raced across the meadow!
But he was too late. Tortoise had won the race.
Hare was the first to congratulate Tortoise.

"Well done, Tortoise!" he said. "You have won because you went steadily along and did not waste time. I can run faster, much faster, than anyone else, so I took it easy. I even fell asleep! It was my own fault that I lost."

"Well, let that be a lesson to us all," said the wise old badger.

Then the tired animals packed up their bags and picnic baskets and went home.